Twas The Night Before Christmas

Clement C. Moore

illustrated by Elena Almazova & Vitaly Shvarov

Grafton and Scratch

PUBLISHERS

'Twas the night before Christmas,
when all through the house,
not a creature was stirring,
not even a mouse.

The stockings were hung
by the chimney with care,
in hopes that St. Nicholas
soon would be there.

The children were nestled
all snug in their beds,
while visions of sugar plums
danced in their heads.

And Mama in her kerchief,
and I in my cap,
had just settled down
for a long winter's nap.
When out on the lawn
there arose such a clatter,
I sprang from the bed
to see what was the matter.

Away to the window I flew like a flash,
tore open the shutters and threw up the sash.

The moon on the crest of the new-fallen snow,
gave the lustre of midday to objects below.
When, what to my wondering eyes should appear,
but a miniature sleigh, and eight tiny reindeer.

With a little old driver, so lively and quick,
I knew in a moment it must be St. Nick.

More rapid than eagles his coursers they came,
and he whistled, and shouted, and called them by name.

"Now Dasher, now Dancer, now Prancer and Vixen!
On Comet, on Cupid, on Donner and Blitzen!
To the top of the porch, to the top of the wall!
Now dash away, dash away, dash away all!"

As dry leaves that before the wild hurricane fly,
when they meet with an obstacle, mount to the sky,
so up to the house-top the coursers they flew,
with a sleigh full of toys and St. Nicholas too.

And then in a twinkling, I heard on the roof,
the prancing and pawing of each little hoof.
As I drew in my head, and was turning around,
down the chimney St. Nicholas came with a bound.

He was dressed all in fur, from his head to his foot,
and his clothes were all tarnished with ashes and soot.

A bundle of toys he had flung on his back,
and he looked like a peddler just opening his pack.

His eyes how they twinkled!
His dimples how merry!
His cheeks were like roses,
his nose like a cherry!
His droll little mouth
was drawn up like a bow,
and the beard of his chin
was as white as the snow.

He had a broad face and a little round belly,
that shook when he laughed, like a bowlful of jelly.

He was chubby and plump, a right jolly old elf
and I laughed when I saw him, in spite of myself.
A wink of his eye and a twist of his head,
soon gave me to know I had nothing to dread.

He spoke not a word, but went straight to his work,
and filled all the stockings, then turned with a jerk,

and laying his finger aside of his nose,
and giving a nod, up the chimney he rose.

He sprang to his sleigh, to his team gave a whistle,
and away they all flew like the down of a thistle.
But I heard him exclaim, as he drove out of sight,

"Happy Christmas to all, and to all a good night."

Published simultaneously in the USA and in Canada in 2012 by Grafton and Scratch Publishers AtlasBooks Distribution

Contact us by e-mail:

publisher@TwasTheNightBeforeChristmas.ca

Visit us:

www.TwasTheNightBeforeChristmas.ca
www.BooksThatFit.com
www.goodreads.com

Also available in e-book formats, including enhanced version with audio and interaction. A softcover edition is available for nonprofit agencies through the offices of the publisher.

Follow us @twas4kids

Find us
www.facebook.com/TwasTheNightBeforeChristmas

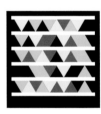

Illustrations copyright © 2012 by
Elena Almazova and Vitaly Shvarov

Printed in Canada on FSC ® certified paper made by New Page, Wisconsin, USA.

10 9 8 7 6 5 4 3 2 1

Book design by Elisa Gutiérrez

LIBRARY AND ARCHIVES CANADA CATALOGUING IN PUBLICATION

Moore, Clement Clarke, 1779-1863
    Twas the night before
Christmas / Clement C. Moore ; edited
by Santa Claus for the benefit of children of the 21st century.

Issued also in electronic format.
ISBN 978-0-9879023-0-6 (bound).--ISBN 978-0-9879023-1-3 (pbk.)

    I. Title.

PS2429.M5N5
2012   j811'.2   C2012-901278-5

LIBRARY AND ARCHIVES CANADA CATALOGUING IN PUBLICATION

Moore, Clement Clarke, 1779-1863
    Twas the night before
Christmas [electronic resource] / Clement
C. Moore ; edited by Santa Claus for the benefit of children of the 21st century.

Electronic monograph.
Issued also in print format.
ISBN 978-0-9879023-2-0 (ebook).--ISBN 978-0-9879023-3-7 (PDF)

    I. Title.

PS2429.M5N5
2012   j811'.2   C2012-901279-3

A gentle Footprint! This book was printed on 100% ancient forest-friendly paper certified by the Forest Stewardship Council (FSC) and printed with vegetable-based inks.